Hans Jürgen Press

The Black Hand Gang and the Treasure in Breezy Lake

Von Jürgen Press
sind in den Ravensburger Taschenbüchern
erschienen:

RTB 52028
Die Abenteuer der „schwarzen hand“

RTB 52066
The Black Hand Gang
and the Mysterious House

RTB 52067
The Black Hand Gang
and the Treasure in Breezy Lake

Hans Jürgen Press

The Black Hand Gang

and the Treasure in Breezy Lake

Illustrations by the author

Ravensburger

Als Ravensburger Taschenbuch
Band 52067
erschienen 1997
Erstmals in den Ravensburger
Taschenbüchern erschienen 1978
(als RTB 505)

Die Abenteuer der „schwarzen hand“
wurden unter Mitarbeit von Fritz Raab im
STERNCHEN, der Kinderbeilage des
STERN Magazins, erstmals veröffentlicht.

Die deutsche Originalausgabe erschien 1965
als RTB – Ravensburger Taschenbuch

Die englische Erstausgabe erschien 1976
bei Methuen Children’s Books Ltd., London

Aus dem Deutschen von Barbara Littlewood
Bearbeitung: Uwe Lüer

Umschlagillustration: Hans Jürgen Press

Printed in Germany

15 16 17 18 19 E D C B A

ISBN 978-3-473-52067-1

www.ravensburger.de

CONTENTS

Introduction

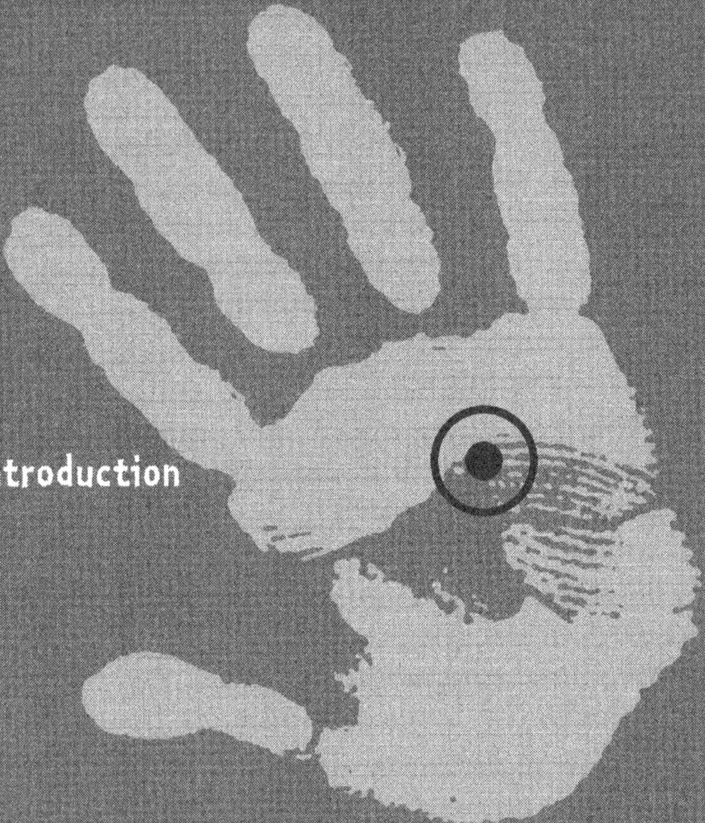

to take a stroll	– einen Streifengang machen
to stare at	= to look at
faded	– verblichen
to pin to	– anheften an
handprint	– Handabdruck
sergeant	– Wachtmeister
to get up to some funny tricks	– lustige Einfälle haben
kids	= children
gang	– Bande
to track down	– zur Strecke bringen
creaking	– krächzend
pigeon loft	– Taubenschlag
leader	– Anführer
quick-witted	– schlagfertig, aufgeweckt
inseparable	– unzertrennlich
squirrel	– Eichhörnchen
locally	= in the place where they live
sleuths	= detectives
case	= Fall
to enable	– befähigen, in die Lage verserzen
skill	– Geschicklichkeit
clue	– hier: Spur, Hinweis
trail	– Fährte
to mark down	= to write down
to check	– überprüfen, auswerten
score	– Punktzahl Trefferzahl

Police Sergeant Shorthouse was taking a stroll along Canal Street, when he paused for a moment in the doorway of Number 49 and stared at a faded notice pinned to the doorpost. It was a piece of paper with a black handprint. The sergeant shook his head and smiled.

“Children really do get up to some funny tricks these days,” he murmured, half to himself. He was thinking of a group of kids who called themselves “The Black Hand Gang” and of the clever way that they had learned to track down criminals.

At the top of this house, up seventy-two creaking stairs, was their clubroom, called the “Airport”, just under the pigeon loft on the roof. The Black Hand Gang met there regularly after school. Frank, who played the trumpet, was the leader; then there was quick-witted Angela; Ralph, who usually wore a striped sweater; and lastly Keith W. S. and his inseparable companion, a squirrel. (W. S. stands for “With Squirrel”.)

The Black Hand Gang’s adventures had made them well known locally as amateur sleuths. This book tells about two cases of their successful career as detectives, and will enable you, the reader, to try your skill at discovering the clues.

⊙→ You can follow the trail by looking carefully at the illustrations. When you have found the right answer, mark it down on a piece of paper, and check your score on the last page.

The Treasure in Breezy Lake

I A Night Visitor

One afternoon at a quarter to three, the door of the local police station burst open and an elderly woman stormed in.
"Sergeant, you must come with me at once. All my jewellery was stolen last night."
"Then, please, take a seat for a moment, madam," Sergeant Shorthouse said and turned back to the Black Hand Gang. "You see, my friends, there's no end of business. But it has been very nice of you to come and see me, and I hope you'll soon come again. And once more: My compliments for your way of solving that difficult smuggler's case. Perhaps ..."
"Is there no one here you can send, Sergeant?" the woman interrupted from her corner.
"I'm afraid that everyone is out at the moment, madam. May I have your name?"
"Ida Partridge; I'm a widow."
"Well, first you must make out a formal complaint."
When Mrs Partridge left the police station some ten minutes later, the Black Hand Gang was waiting for her on the steps.
Frank said, "Don't worry, Mrs Partridge, we'll help you."
Then they all went off to view the scene of the crime.
"What a dreadful mess he's made,' said Angela, "but at least we know exactly what time he was here."

How did the gang know when the burglary had taken place?

treasure	– Schatz	crime	– Verbrechen
complaint	– hier: Anzeige	dreadful	– fürchterlich
to view	– anschauen	burglary	– Einbruch

NO ENTRY
WARNING
WANTED
POLICE STATION

2 A Clue on the Roof

"Mrs Partridge's clock stopped at exactly five minutes past midnight," Angela said. "The burglar was probably looking for a safe." Mrs Partridge handed round a packet of fruit gums. Ralph added: "He must have come in by the balcony window – look, one of the panes is broken."

The Black Hand Gang went out on to the balcony to search for clues. "Not the smallest trace," said Ralph. He peered at the edge of the roof through his magnifying glass.

"Our cat burglar must have climbed over the roof," Frank remarked. Keith W.S. stroked his squirrel and murmured, as he put it on the roof, "Here's a job for you, little friend."

After a few seconds the squirrel began scratching in the gutter, then picked up something in its paws.

Ralph shouted, "It's a cinema ticket. Here's our first clue."

Angela, twitching her plaits, asked: "Which film had he gone to see?"

The Black Hand Gang bought a newspaper on their way back to the Airport and looked at the cinema advertisements. It wasn't an easy task. Frank was the first to work it out.

"He chose the right film," he said, doubling up with laughter.

What was the film called?

clue	– Spur, Beweis	to peer	– spähen
fruit gums	– Gummibären, Kaubonbons	gutter	– Dachrinne
pane	– Fensterscheibe	to twitch	– drehen
trace	– Spur	plaits	– Zöpfe
magnifying glass	– Vergrößerungsglas	advertisement	– Anzeige, Reklame
		task	– Aufgabe
		to double up with	– sich biegen vor

ALACE
Street Tel. 27338
Seat 11
talls
Row H
21.00 hours
7th May
to be retained
FILM TIMETABLE
7th May
SAVOY CINEMA. Showing at 18.30 & 21.00. The Cowboys. Long Eaton Street. Tel. 32111
TIVOLI. Canal St. Tel. 27090. 16.00. 18.30, 21.00. Festival of Sport. Closed on Sunday.
CRYSTAL PALACE. George Steel in Night of Terror. 'A' 18.15, 20.45, King St. Tel. 28379
Bill Day Presents
THE SNOW MONSTER
Sensational Film
A
18.30 21.00
GLORY PALACE
Brille Square. Tel. 25203
Mr. X in Par
Pierre Carlo
Mimi Duval
HIPP
Telephone: Central 57620
Anita Rushwell and Fabian Strong in a breath-taking film
THE CLOCK STRUCK TWELVE
16.00, 18.30, 20.45
Royal Square. Tel. 31121
"The Film of The Year"
Daily Echo
Metropol
super Cinema
Jean Benton
Bob Telfer
Good Evening My Lord
URANIA
Tel. 47812
18.15 20.45
Victim of Frankenstein
90min of HORROR
capitol
Bridge St. Tel. 27222
A
12th WEEK
ATHENIUM. Tel. 37123
Moon. 18.00, 21.00
Parkway Road.
GRAND PLAZA. 55, York Road. Don't Count Your Chickens. 'U' Cartoon. 18.30, 21.00. Tel. 21307
PICTURE HOUSE. Central St. The Adventures of Fred Fox. 'U' 18.30 only. Tel. 27739
CINEMA PALACE. Stirling St. Deep Pockets-Long Fingers. 16.00, 18.30, 21.00. Tel. 27338
NEW ASTORIA. Vine Grove. Comedy Capers. All star cast. 18.00, 20.00. Tel. 24187
STUDIO
18.15 20.30
The Indian Chief
16.00 18.30 21.00
BIG CHIEF EAGLE EYE
Town Hall Square

3 The Other Side

“Deep pockets – long fingers” was the title of the film. Angela turned the ticket over. “Look at this!” she exclaimed. The Gang read it out in unison: “... aser”.
“It must be part of someone’s name,” said Frank. “He must have booked his seat in advance.”
“He’s probably a regular cinema-goer,” added Angela.
The following evening the Black Hand Gang went to the cinema and loitered by the ticket office, hoping that someone would eventually ask for “aser’s” tickets. The only result was that the commissionaire came to shoo them away.
“But we’re the Black Hand Gang,” said Angela.
“Not the gang the newspapers were talking about the other day ...” “Yes, we’re the ones,” said Angela proudly.
So the commissionaire was only too pleased to let them stay.
Three evenings later their luck was in. A man and a woman in motor-cycle gear came up to the ticket window.
“Tickets for Fraser?” the man asked. The commissionaire managed to get four seats in the front row for the Black Hand Gang.
“We must stay close to our suspects,” said Frank. “Did anyone notice which seats they took?”
After about half an hour Keith W. S. said: “There they are.”

Which row were the suspects in?

in unison	– gleichzeitig	commissionaire	– Portier
to book	– buchen, vorbestellen	to shoo away	– fortscheuchen
		their luck was in	– sie hatten Glück
in advance	– im Voraus	gear	– Kleidung
probably	– vermutlich	front row	– vordere Reihe
to loiter	– herumschlendern	suspects	– Verdächtige

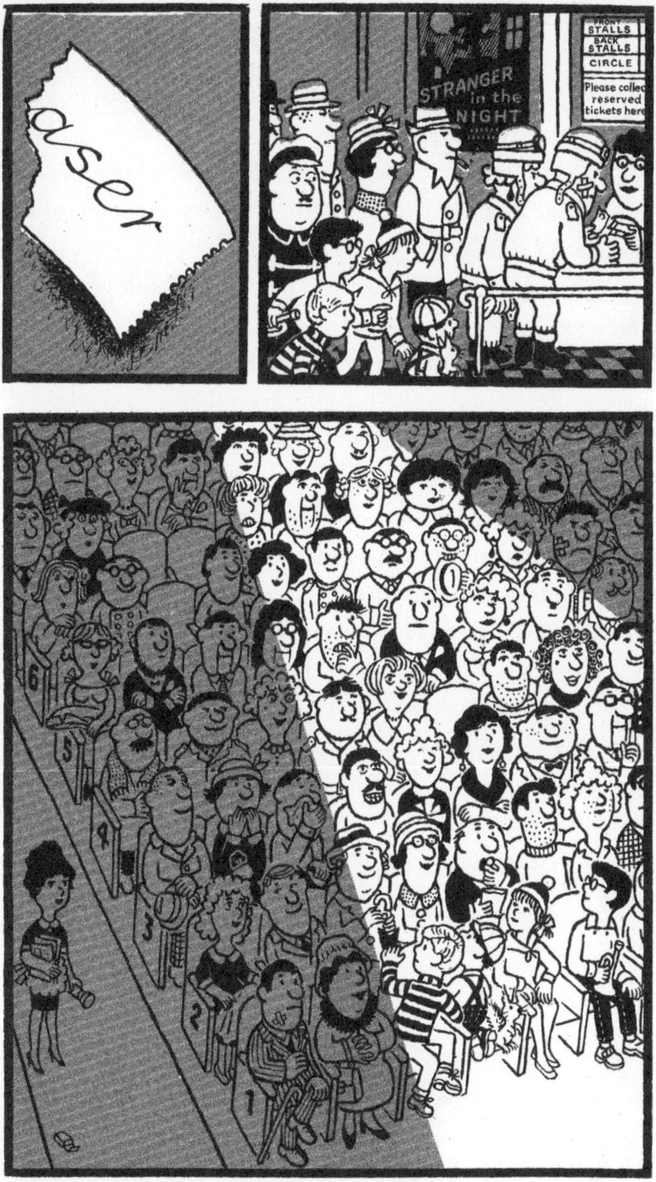
aser
STRANGER in the NIGHT
FRONT STALLS
BACK STALLS
CIRCLE
Please collec
reserved
tickets here

4 Mobile Unit

Once the Black Hand Gang had spotted the motorcyclists sitting in the sixth row, they slipped out of the cinema and held an urgent conference outside. “We must find out where Fraser lives,” said Ralph. Angela asked: “How are we going to do that?” – “We’ll follow him on our bikes.”

The Black Hand Gang separated. Angela, Keith W.S. and Ralph went to watch the three exits and Frank the car park. At about half past ten the audience began to stream out, and a few minutes later came Frank’s trumpet signal. They pedalled off furiously, swept round the corner into East Street in the wake of the motor-cycle. Fraser accelerated away, though, and the Black Hand Gang lost him. They could still hear the throbbing of his engine, but then the noise suddenly stopped.

“He can’t be far,” called Frank. “Let’s look for the motor-cycle. Its number is PXE 1314.” They soon found it parked in front of Number 28, Windmill Street. The Black Hand Gang looked for Fraser’s name on the nameplates beside the street door.

“Bother,” said Angela. “Fraser isn’t here.”

Just then Frank strolled up, looking very pleased with himself. “Fraser does live here,” he said. “I’ve seen his name.”

Where had Frank seen the name?

mobile unit	– Rollkommando	to pedal off	– in die Pedale treten
to spot	– entdecken	to sweep	– fegen, jagen
to slip out	– sich hinausstehlen	wake	– Kielwasser
urgent	– dringend	to accelerate	– Gas geben
to separate	– sich trennen	though	– jedoch
exit	– Ausgang	throbbing	– Dröhnen
car park	– Parkplatz	to stroll up	– heranschlendern
audience	– Zuschauer		
to stream	– strömen		

KENYAN
COFFEE

Gray
Barrie
Pool
Edwards
Fraser
BESPOKE
TAILOR
PX
E 1314

5 The Locked Door

Frank had seen the name on a letter-box near by.
"Well," said Angela, "let's go and brave the wolf in his den."
"Let's wait till daylight," Frank suggested.
When they came back to Windmill Street the next morning, the motor-cycle had disappeared. They went into the house and found Fraser's flat up in the attic. Ralph rang the bell. No one answered. Frank tried to look through the keyhole, but it was blocked. "Let me try," said Angela, and she waggled the door-handle. The door was locked, but they heard a voice calling: "I'm ill in bed. Please go away and leave me in peace."
"Strange enough," said Ralph pressing the handle, too. "There's no answer to our ringing, only a voice when the handle is down. Listen!" And again there was the voice: "I'm ill in bed. Leave me in peace!"
Ralph had already taken his special penknife with its seventeen different attachments out of his pocket and was unscrewing the handle. He pulled it off and pushed it through the other side, so that he had a peep hole. He put his eye to it and whispered to the others, "The bed's empty."
Angela had a look, too, and said: "Fraser isn't there, but I know where his voice is coming from."

Where was Fraser's voice coming from?

to brave the wolf in his den (= engl. Sprichwort)	– in die Höhle des Löwen gehen	doorhandle	– Türklinke
flat	– Wohnung	penknife	– Taschenmesser
attic	– Dachboden	attachment	– Werkzeug, Vorrichtung
to waggle	– hier: wackeln	to unscrew	– abschrauben
		peep hole	– Guckloch

FRASER

6 The Bird Flies into the Nest

Fraser's voice had come from a tape-recorder under the bed.
"He's gone away," said Angela. "What are we going to do now?"
"We know the number of his motor-cycle," said Ralph.
"That's no use," Keith W. S. said. "This case is hopeless."
"Look here," Frank said, "we're not giving up as easily as that. We'll keep looking, all of us."
Days went by. The Black Hand Gang searched streets, backyards, car parks, but found no trace. They began to comb the surrounding villages, too, but Fraser and his motor-cycle had completely vanished.
Ralph was ready to give up the search when Fate lent a hand. One afternoon as they were riding round the countryside Frank suddenly braked hard. "Look, there," he shouted.
Half hidden in the bushes was the motor-cycle with the PXE 1314 number plate. "The rear wheel is missing," Angela noticed. "And where is its rider?" asked Keith W. S. "He must be near here." The Gang looked around.
"Come on!" exclaimed Frank, running towards a nearby camp site. It was only a matter of seconds before he pointed towards one of the tents. "That's our man. See what he's doing."

What was Fraser doing?

tape-recorder	– Tonbandgerät	Fate	– das Schicksal
no use	– nutzlos	to lend a hand	– mithelfen
backyard	– Hinterhof	to brake	– bremsen
trace	– Spur	number plate	– Nummernschild
to comb	– durchkämmen	rear wheel	– Hinterrad
to vanish	– verschwinden	camp site	– Campingplatz

CAMP SITE

NO HEAVY LORRIES ON THE SITE
NO LITTER PLEASE
CAR PARK

7 Frogmen

Fraser was pumping up his tyre. But what on earth was he doing in a camping site near Breezy Lake?

"Do you think he realized that we were following him?" suggested Ralph.

"Anyhow, we must keep a close watch on him from now on," said Frank.

They settled down on a small hill from which they could observe Fraser's tent. For two hours nothing happened except for ants biting them all over. But at moonrise Fraser stole out of his tent and crept down to the shore. He threw a heavy object, to which a rope was attached, into the lake. The Gang heard it splash. Fraser returned noiselessly to his tent.

"What can that have been?" Angela whispered.

"Tomorrow we'll go and look," Frank answered.

The next day the Gang were back, equipped with flippers and masks.

After several attempts of diving they found what they thought was the right place and dived again. Suddenly Frank signalled to them to surface. He had discovered what Fraser had thrown into the lake.

What had Fraser thrown into the lake?

frogman	– Froschmann, Taucher	ant	– Ameise
to pump up	– aufpumpen	rope	– Leine
tyre	– Reifen	to attach	– festmachen
to realize	– (be)merken	lake	– See
to keep a close watch	– genau beobachten	to equip	– ausstatten
		flipper	– Flosse
		attempt	– Versuch
to settle	– sich niederlassen	to surface	– auftauchen
to observe	– beobachten	to signal	– signalisieren

8 The Necklace

Frank had spotted a bag at the bottom of the lake.
"Are you sure it belongs to Fraser?" Angela asked.
"It must do. There's a rope attached to it," Frank said. "Let's go down again and see what it contains."
When they reached the bag Ralph opened the knots and Frank pulled out a necklace. At that moment there was a sharp tug on the rope and the bag vanished upwards. The gang realized at once that Fraser had returned. They surfaced among the reeds.
"What a nuisance!" Ralph exclaimed, furiously.
"At least we have recovered a necklace," Frank said, trying to cheer him up.
Angela inspected it. "It looks like a family heirloom," she said.
An hour later they stood outside Mrs Partridge's door. She was far from happy.
It's disgraceful," she complained. "The police still haven't found my jewellery."
"We may have good news for you," Angela interrupted. "We have found something and we'd like you to tell us if it belongs to you. Show her the necklace, Frank."
"No need," answered Frank. "I know it is her necklace."

How did Frank know the necklace belonged to Mrs Partridge?

necklace	– Halskette	to recover	– wieder finden
bottom	– Grund	to cheer up	– aufmuntern
to contain	– enthalten	heirloom	– Erbstück
tug	– Ruck	disgraceful	– schändlich
reed	– Schilf	jewellery	– Schmuck
what a nuisance	– wie ärgerlich	to complain	– sich beklagen
furiously	– wütend		

9 One Step Behind

As soon as Frank pointed out the necklace in the painting, he said to the others: "Quick, let's get back to Breezy Lake. Hurry." They were, of course, just too late. Fraser had left on his motor-cycle.

"We'll have to tell Sergeant Shorthouse," said Ralph. "I'll call him."

A short time later a squealing of brakes announced the arrival of a police car at Breezy Lake. The Black Hand Gang jumped in and they raced off again, Angela explaining the position to the Sergeant as they went. "Stop!" she shouted suddenly. The car drew up beside a policeman on a bicycle.

"A motor-cycle and side-car? Yes, I've seen one. It turned into Robertson's farm a little while ago."

As they entered the farmyard with the police, the Black Hand Gang saw the motor-cycle. They went into the house and called, "Hello."

"Yeeees," answered a woman's voice from the kitchen.

"That's his girl friend," whispered Frank. "The one he took to the cinema that evening."

"What's your name?" asked Sergeant Shorthouse.

"Rita Fergusson. I'm the cleaning woman. The boss and his wife have gone to town. I've been here alone all morning."

"She's lying," Ralph said. "There's the proof."

What had Ralph seen?

to point out	– hinweisen auf	to race off	– davonrasen
painting	– Bild, Gemälde	cleaning woman	– Putzfrau
squealing	– Quietschen	proof	– Beweis

POLICE
DON'T COUNT YOUR CHICKENS BEFORE THEYRE HATCHED
SUGAR
FLOU
SALT

10 Rita Won't Talk

Sergeant Shorthouse held the smoking cheroot under Rita's nose and asked sternly: "Where is the man hiding?"
"I don't know what you're talking about."
"If that's the way you want it," the Sergeant answered, "we'll search the whole house. Show us round."
Rita pulled a chair into the middle of the room and sat down on it, saying with a scornful air, "Search if you want to. Go and creep down every little mousehole, but don't expect me to help you."
Sergeant Shorthouse wasted no more time but took his men to search every room in the house. Meanwhile, the Black Hand Gang sat on the stairs and watched Rita closely.
"If they can't find Fraser," Keith W.S. whispered, "they'll think it's our fault."
"He must be here," answered Frank.
At last only the store cupboards remained and Sergeant Shorthouse inspected these too, without result. He came back to the children and said, "Well, we've looked everywhere ..."
"There's one door you've missed," Angela answered. "Perhaps that's the right one."

Which door did Angela mean?

cheroot	– Stumpen	with a scornful air	– in verächtlichem Ton
sternly	– streng	fault	– Fehler, Schuld
to search	– durchsuchen	store cupboards	– Vorratsschränke

11 The Last Door

Sergeant Shorthouse did not see the trap door before Angela pointed it out. "Get up," he snapped at Rita. As he pulled the door open she cried, "There's really no one down there."
Sergeant Shorthouse only laughed and shouted down into the cellar: "Come out of there, no one."
A crash helmet slowly emerged and under it, a face.
"Fraser!" exclaimed the Gang with one voice.
Sergeant Shorthouse put the handcuffs on him and asked, "Where's the loot?" But Fraser struggled furiously and said, "I'll sue you. I'm an honest man."
"That remains to be seen."
The second policeman climbed down to the cellar and returned with the bag. "There's nothing else suspicious," he said.
Sergeant Shorthouse reached into the bag. It was empty.
"Mr Fraser was just bringing up some potatoes for me," Rita said, angrily. "Your arrival upset him."
She said much more besides, not noticing that the Black Hand Gang had slipped quietly away into the cellar.
Ralph, squinting in the gloom, suddenly exclaimed: "I've found it. Look, all of you, there's the stolen jewellery!"

Where was the jewellery?

trap door	– Bodenklappe	that remains to be seen	– das wird sich zeigen
to snap at	– anschnauzen	suspicious	– verdächtig
crash helmet	– Sturzhelm	to upset	– verwirren
to emerge	– hervorkommen	to squint	– herumgucken, blinzeln
handcuffs	– Handschellen	gloom	– Dunkelheit
loot	– Beute		
to sue	– verklagen		

12 The Finder's Reward

The following Saturday, when the Gang was cycling through the city, Angela had the idea to take their way along King's Road where Mrs Partridge lived.

"She's at home." Ralph was the first to discover her sitting on her balcony under a yellow sunshade. "Let's go up to her and see how she's doing."

Mrs Partridge had heard their voices from afar and waited to welcome them. "I knew you would come," she said cheerfully. "Sergeant Shorthouse has been here, too; and he told me where you've found my jewellery: in a preserving glass. How clever of you!"

"Then there's nothing left to do for us?" Angela asked.

"Yes, there is." Mrs Partridge smiled, and from her sideboard she took five nuts. "Here are some more nuts for you to crack!"

The squirrel at once started doing so. But not before they had come home did the others notice that their nuts had been treated. And what was inside? A theatre ticket for each of them with a note on the reverse side:

Thank you very much. Ida Partridge.

to cycle	– Rad fahren	to treat	– präparieren
preserving glass	– Einmachglas	reverse side	– Rückseite
but not before ...	– aber erst als ...		

A Theft at the Zoo

I A Photograph of the Scene of the Crime

All's well that ends well: It was a lovely day when the Black Hand Gang went back home by train after wonderful holidays. But perhaps this was the reason why their spirits were not too high. Who would like going home when school will begin soon? Their talks began flagging and they sat listlessly watching the landscape pass by. The only one who jumped about happily was the squirrel. When they had almost reached home Ralph spotted a newsman who was shouting the latest headlines: "Theft at the zoo. Black panther stolen!" He sprang to the window and shouted: "Hi there, a paper, please!"
The news raised their spirits immediately. Angela spread the paper on the bench. "That's an interesting story," she said after a while. "Besides, it seems to be about that rare little panther in our own zoo."
"It sounds like our sort of case," suggested Ralph.
Keith W.S. objected. "But it says already that there are no clues. We'd just make ourselves look silly."
Ralph, however, was studying the photograph through his magnifying glass. Suddenly he looked more closely. "I've just found our first clue," he said. "Look! The thief has dropped something."

What had the thief dropped?

high spirits	– gute Stimmung	to raise	– heben; verbessern
to flag	– stocken, weniger werden	to object	– Einspruch erheben
theft	– Diebstahl		
spirits	– Geister; Stimmung		

zookeeper
discovered
Panther, or
a mystery
must not
is found
e Police
trouble
tioning
to be
e Zoo
s not
king
way
nat Here is the empty cage where
or Ernesto, the Panther cub, lived.
te Police investigating the theft
el found the door locked. The thief
y apparently left no clues a
it is a mystery how
Zoo
82
BLACK
PANTHER
Felis Pardus
DO NOT
FEED

2 A Long Arm

That same afternoon the Black Hand Gang cycled off to the zoo and went straight to the panther's cage. Angela began to search under the little bush where she soon found the key that Ralph had discovered in the newspaper photograph.

"We knew we should find this," she said, "and now we must establish where it came from."

When they showed the key to the keeper, he stared and stared. "I simply don't believe it. Where did you find that?"

The Black Hand Gang introduced themselves and explained how they had come across it.

"Ah! I've heard of you. My name, by the way, is Winterton. I do hope you'll discover what has become of poor Ernesto." Mr Winterton led them into the keepers' lodge and showed them the board where the keys usually hung.

"Was the door locked?" asked Ralph.

"Of course. We have a safety lock."

"What about the window?"

"That was only latched, but no one could get through the bars."

"Only a person with arms two yards long," said Angela, laughing.

Suddenly Keith W. S. interrupted. "That's just what he did have and I can see how he managed it."

How did the thief take the key?

to establish	– hier: feststellen	safety lock	– Sicherheitsschloss
to come across	– stoßen auf	to latch	– anlehnen
lodge	– Pförtnerloge	bars	– Gitter

KEEPER'S OFFICE
ZOO
9
KEEPER'S
OFFICE
NO
ENTRY

3 A Comb

It can't have been difficult for the thief to reach the key with the hook on the handle of the rake.
"This was a professional job," Keith W. S. stated finally. "Who has been the last to use the rake?" asked Angela.
Mr Winterton thought for a minute. "It must have been our new gardener. He was mowing the lawn here yesterday."
Keith W.S. bent down to examine the grass when he suddenly shouted: "Look at this!"
"This" was a pocket comb with the trade name *Delux* on it.
"That probably belongs to the thief," said Angela.
"Or to the gardener," Keith W. S. suggested.
"They may be one and the same person."
They went off to find the gardener who was mowing the grass in the dinosaur park.
"What can I do for you, then?" he asked, wiping the sweat from his forehead.
"We wondered whether you had lost something," said Frank.
"Me? No, I don't think so. I haven't noticed anything missing."
Ralph grinned: "No. I can see now that you haven't."

Why were they sure that it wasn't the gardener's comb?

rake	– Rechen, Harke	trade name	– Warenzeichen
professional	– von einem Fachmann	to suggest	– vorschlagen, meinen
to state	– feststellen	sweat	– Schweiß
to mow	– mähen	to grin	– grinsen
lawn	– Rasen		

DELUX
Tyranno-
saurus

4 A Scream

“A bald-headed man doesn’t need a comb,” said Angela.
“Then who lost it?” asked Ralph gazing once again at the comb through his magnifying glass. A curly black hair was caught in its teeth.
“Perhaps we can learn something from that,” said Frank, putting both comb and hair into an envelope.
“What shall we do now?” asked Keith W. S.
“Go and take shelter,” answered Angela.
It had begun to rain, so they went to the door of the elephant house. They had been there for about half an hour when a scream shrilled through the air. Then a great number of voices began to bicker and screech. The Black Hand Gang looked sharply about them.
“Over there!” Frank shouted, pointing to one of the buildings. They ran towards it and found themselves in the parrot house. Frank looked about him swiftly, then pointed to the cage door.
“He’s sawn through the lock,” he said curtly. “Look at the feathers on the ground.”
“Do you think one of the birds has been stolen?” Angela asked.
“Undoubtedly,” put in Keith W. S. “One has been taken and I know its name.”

What was the stolen parrot called?

bald-headed	– kahlköpfig	to screech	– kreischen
to gaze at	– genau anschauen	parrot	– Papagei
magnifying glass	– Vergrößerungsglas	swiftly	– rasch
shelter	– Unterschlupf	to saw (sawed, sawn)	– sägen
to shrill	– gellen	feather	– Feder
to bicker	– zetern	undoubtedly	– ohne Zweifel

TALKING BIRDS
CARL
MAX
LAURA
RALPH
CLARA
LOLA
MIMI
TOTO

5 "Here's Clara"

The stolen parrot was called Clara. "This is very bad luck," said Mr Winterton. "She was the best talker we had."
"What are we going to do now?" asked Angela.
The Black Hand Gang thought hard.
"A talking parrot is difficult to dispose of," said Keith W.S.
"That's right," Ralph agreed. "If the thief keeps her he'll give himself away."
"That means he must get her out of town as quickly as possible," Keith W.S. argued. "Most likely by train."
Frank clasped his head in his hands. "Why didn't I think of that before. Let's go to the station."
The evening mail was just being loaded on to the train as the Black Hand Gang arrived. They pushed their way through the post trolleys, calling softly: "Clara, Clara."
"No one called Clara here," grunted a porter.
The children were just about to explain to him what Clara was when a faint sound caught their ear. Softly but distinctly, a voice had said: "Here's Clara. Here's Clara." The Gang hesitated only for a second. Then Ralph pointed.
"Clara must be in there," he said. "What a curious name and address."

To whom was the package addressed?

bad luck	– Unglück, Jammer	mail	– Post(sendung)
to dispose of	– loswerden, beseitigen	trolley	– Wagen
to give oneself away	– sich verraten	to grunt	– brummen
likely	– wahrscheinlich	faint	– schwach
to clasp	– hier: halten, stützen	to catch the ear	– zu hören sein
		to hesitate	– zögern
		package	– Paket

371
51
EXPRESS
335
HANDLE WITH CARE
This Way UP
440
First Class
349
Second Class
FRAGILE
GLASS
314
F. Nikel & Co. Lt
553
CHUBBY Dog food
TOP
410
421
First Class
Second Class
UP!
This Way UP
GLASS
429
391
Handle With Care
388
Handle With
FRAGILE
Livestock With Care
LORD CARO
Poste restante
EXPRESS
To The Airport
This way up
BONZ LTD
This Way up
333
Express
First Class
515
521
Warmer Wool Co. Limited
513
78

6 A Telephone Conversation

"Lord Caro is a very odd name," said Angela. "I think it's a pseudonym," Frank replied. "Should we go to Loverton?"
"Why should we?" Keith W.S. asked. "It would be simpler to telephone."
A few minutes later they had found a phone box. Frank dialled the number of the Loverton exchange and asked if there was anyone called Lord Caro living in the town.
"Just a moment please." This moment lasted about three minutes and, as it was a trunk call, Angela had to put two more coins into the slot. "This is too expensive," she complained.
"Hush," said Frank, listening to the voice at the other end.
He said "Thank you" and replaced the receiver. Then he said to the others, "A complete waste of time. They say no one of that name lives in Loverton." Someone knocked sharply on the glass. "How long are you going to be in there?" asked a man impatiently. "Please do come in, Sir," said Keith W.S. with mock politeness. "We have quite finished now." As they came out he poked Frank in the ribs. "Lord Caro will be visiting Newtown in person shortly."
"How do you know that?"
Keith W.S. smiled. "He has business here."

What was Lord Caro's profession?

odd	– komisch	slot	– Einwurf, Schlitz
pseudonym	– Künstlername, Deckname	to complain	– sich beklagen
to dial	– wählen	waste of time	– Zeitvergeudung
exchange	– (Fernsprech-) Amt	mock politeness	– mit übertriebener Höflichkeit
trunk call	– Ferngespräch	to poke	– stoßen
coin	– Münze	profession	– Beruf

Use
Engler
Tyres
HOTEL
LAUNDERETTE
TRIXIE'S VARIETY
SHOW
GREAT
SENSATIONAL
ACTS
Starring
LORD
CARO
well
known
magician
From 5-12 August
Daily at 16-00 & 20-00
Many
other
rtistes
DANCING
NIGHTLY
ROXI
FILTER
TELEPHONE
TELEPHONE
PLEASE
BE
QUICK
Local and
Trunk Calls
LOST
Blue
Budgerigar
Please Contact
P. COOPER

7 The Lady Lied

When Trixie's Variety Show including Lord Caro, the magician, arrived in Newtown the Black Hand Gang were on the spot to greet them. They stood unnoticed, watching while the baggage was unpacked. "Let's just ask where Lord Caro is," said Ralph. "No," said Frank. "He'd wonder why we were asking." – "Do you have a better idea, then?"
Angela stepped in. "Let's play stupid," she said.
Strolling up to a heavily made-up woman who was in difficulties with a suitcase and some packing cases, she asked innocently, "Can I help you?" and had the case free at once.
"Thank you."
"What a lot of baggage you have," said Angela, pretending to be astonished. "Do you have animals, too?"
"Yes. Rabbits and doves."
"Wild animals?" Angela was thinking of the little panther that had been stolen from the zoo. The woman gave her a searching stare, then said curtly, "No" and walked away.
"I'm sure she was lying," Angela told the others.
"You could be right," said Frank, "but we have no proof."
"I think we have," said Ralph. "Read that notice."

What had Ralph seen?

to lie, lied, lied	– lügen	innocently	– unschuldig
including	– samt	to pretend	– vortäuschen
magician	– Zauberkünstler	to give a searching stare	– forschend anblicken
on the spot	– zur Stelle	curtly	– schroff
unnoticed	– unbeobachtet	to bet	– wetten
baggage	– Gepäck	props	– Requisiten
heavily made-up	– aufgedonnert	vicious	– bösartig
to be in difficulties	– Schwierigkeiten haben	inflammable	– brennbar

SILENCE
STAGE DOOR
No Smoking
Mind The Step
DANGER Inflammable Material
WARNING VICIOUS ANIMAL
Make-up
9
PROPS
COLA Refreshes

8 Sir Henry

No one would put "WARNING Vicious Animal" on a cage full of bunny rabbits," said Ralph.

"Let's go and watch the show tomorrow afternoon," Frank suggested.

It was 4 o'clock when the curtain went up on Lord Caro, Magician. Keith W. S. thought immediately of Clara when he saw the bird on the stand and so did the others. But how could they tell if it was really Clara?

"Ladies and Gentlemen!" Lord Caro cleared his throat. "May I introduce my assistant Sir Henry." He held a microphone under the bird's beak. "Say hello to the audience, Sir Henry."

"'Allo, 'allo, la'ies an' gen'lemen," squawked a voice from the loudspeaker.

Lord Caro held a long conversation with the bird, and the Black Hand Gang became quite worried. It seemed as if this couldn't be Clara.

Suddenly Frank exclaimed: "That bird hasn't opened its beak once!"

"Is Lord Caro a vetriloquist?" whispered Angela.

"Be quiet," hissed the stout lady sitting next to them.

After a short silence Ralph murmured: "Someone else is doing the voice. Look over there by the loudspeaker cable."

Where was the parrot's voice coming from?

bunny rabbits	– Karnickel	to squawk	– kreischen
to introduce	– vorstellen	ventriloquist	– Bauchredner
beak	– Schnabel	silence	– Stille

EXIT

9 Getting Warm

A pair of shoes was peeping out from under the curtain and betrayed a helper who imitated the parrot's voice.
"We must bring Mr Winterton along to watch," Frank whispered. "He'll be able to recognize Clara." The Gang tiptoed out of the theatre and went to the zoo. The keeper was in the reptile house. "Thank heavens you're here," he cried.
"What's happened?" asked Keith W. S. "Our python, our most valuable snake!" – "Not dead!" said Ralph.
Mr Winterton wiped his forehead. "I've only just come in. I was walking past when I saw someone run out of the reptile house. Naturally I came in and when I saw the damage – the broken glass and the python lying limply on the floor – I sent for Mr Falter, our veterinary surgeon, at once. But I ..."
"We're in luck, Winterton," shouted the vet. "Your python was only stunned."
"How long ago did you see that fellow?" Frank asked.
"About ten minutes ago."
"The trail is still warm then. Come on, let's go and look!" Frank said. While they were examining the ground behind the reptile house for clues, Ralph found something. "Come here," he shouted. "A bottle!"

What did the bottle contain?

to betray	– verraten
to recognize	– (wieder) erkennen
to tiptoe	– auf Zehenspitzen gehen
python(snake)	– Pythonschlange
damage	– Schaden
limply	– schlaff
veterinary surgeon (= vet)	– Tierarzt
stunned	– betäubt
trail	– Spur, Fährte
clue	– Spur, Beweis

Balinese
Temple
Figure
HOTEI
Asian God of
Happiness
Ether
To The
Lions' Enclosure

10 Trick Photography

"Ether is an anaesthetic," said Ralph. "This bottle must belong to the thief."

They all thought quickly.

"Best not to touch anything," said Frank. "The thief will come back for his bottle."

"We can set a trap for him," said Ralph.

The others looked at him in surprise.

"It's quite simple," he went on. "We'll hide a camera in that nest-box and fasten a thread to the shutter. If we fasten the other end to the bottle the thief will photograph himself when he tries to take it away."

"Brilliant!" Frank exclaimed, and Ralph hurried off to fetch his camera.

Half an hour later they set to work.

"Be careful not to spoil any fingerprints," Frank warned.

Angela peered through the magnifying glass. "There aren't any. He wiped them off."

"No, he didn't," said Keith W. S. "He didn't leave any."

"How do you know?"

Keith W. S. pointed. "There's your proof."

What had Keith W.S. found?

ether	– Äther	shutter	– Verschluss
anaesthetic	– Betäubungsmittel	to spoil	– verderben
trap	– Falle	fingerprint	– Fingerabdruck
thread	– Bindfaden		

11 | # In Search of J.N.

Inside the glove that Keith W.S. picked up were printed the letters J.N. This glove was their second evidence.
Next morning Ralph slipped into the zoo on his way to school to see if the photo-trap had sprung. The bottle was gone and the thread hung from the shutter, broken. Trembling with excitement Ralph took the film out of his camera and took it to be developed. That afternoon the Black Hand Gang went to collect it.
"What a disappointment," said Angela sadly. "Only a trouser leg."
"Better than nothing," said Frank. "Let's go back to the zoo."
At the entrance they met Mr Winterton. "Oh, children," he said, "this time the snake really has been stolen. I discovered the theft just ten minutes ago. We're trying to watch everyone who goes out, but you can see for yourselves that it's hopeless."
Frank took the rest of the Gang on one side. "Look," he said, "we know he has dark, curly hair and wears check trousers."
"And that his name begins with J.N." added Keith W.S.
The Black Hand Gang had been watching the crowds for only sixteen minutes when Angela suddenly cried:
"There's our man!"

→ ◯ **Who was the man?**

glove	– Handschuh	to collect	– abholen
evidence	– Beweisstück	theft	– Diebstahl
to spring, sprung	– hier: zuschnappen	curly	– lockig
gone	– hier: verschwunden	check trousers	– karierte Hosen
excitement	– Aufregung	crowd	– (Menschen-) Menge
to develop	– entwickeln		

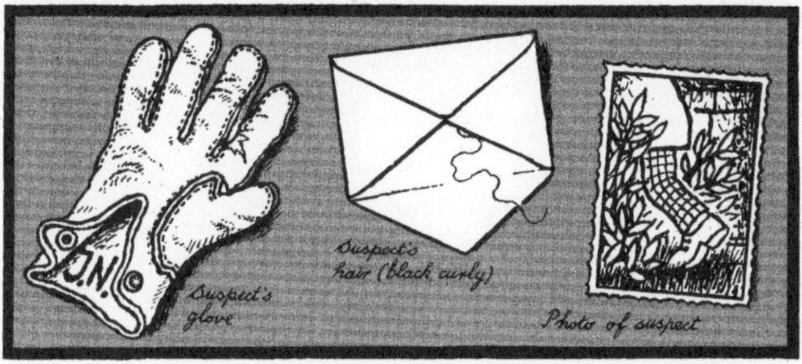
J.N.
Suspect's glove
Suspect's hair (black curly)
Photo of suspect

ZOO
ZOO
ZOO
Hours
From 9.00
TICKET OFFICE
Information
BUS H
EXCURSION
Snapshots
3 POSES
75p
CN
PN
STREET MAP
blatt
ICES
HL
Prop.
J. Nickel

12 Nickel Gives Himself Away

The owner of the ice-cream cart, J. Nickel, fitted the description.

"Right," said Frank. "We'll follow him."

Ralph thought they ought to search the ice-cream cart. "I doubt if that gentleman would agree to that," commented Keith W.S.

"We could buy an ice-cream," Frank suggested.

"Good idea," said Angela.

They ran round to the front of the cart.

"Excuse me," said Angela, "I'd like a vanilla ice, please."

"Sold out," the man replied, and brushed by Angela so closely that he almost knocked her down.

"You pig!" she exclaimed.

The Black Hand Gang waited only a few seconds before following, but when they turned the corner the cart had vanished.

"Now what?" asked Keith W.S., exasperated.

"He must have gone into one of the alleys," said Ralph.

They checked two alleys without finding anything, and went on into the third.

"This is the one," said Ralph. "There, in that building."

What was the number of the house?

to give oneself away	– sich verraten	to brush	– vorbeisausen
cart	– Wagen, Karre	exasperated	– wütend
to fit	– passen (auf)	alley	– hier: Torbogen, Durchfahrt
description	– Beschreibung	to check	– überprüfen
to doubt	– bezweifeln		

ICES

No playing in this entry
43b
43a
LOCK-SMITH
Boot-maker
43c
43d
DOG and CAT Food.

13 Mrs Appleyard Has Got Sharp Ears

Frank went up to Number 43 A and saw the ice-cream cart behind the door. He tried to open the door, but it was locked.
"We'll have to wait until he comes out," he told the others.
But Keith W.S. pointed to the fire escape. "We should be able to see into the window from up there," he said.
The Gang crept quietly up the ladder. When they reached the second platform, Frank signalled to them to be silent, and lay down on his stomach. The others bent down and peered through the ladder.
"Yes, that's Nickel," whispered Ralph. "Who is the woman?"
"It must be the landlady," replied Angela. "Be quiet and we might hear what they're saying."
They could hear quite clearly.
The landlady said, "You have someone in your room, Mr Nickel. You know perfectly well that I don't allow strangers."
Nickel smiled at her.
"It's no use your smiling. I distinctly heard footsteps in your room."
"You must have been dreaming, Mrs Appleyard," answered Nickel.
Angela nudged Ralph. "She wasn't dreaming, the stranger is still there. Look closely."

Where was the visitor?

sharp	– hier: gute	landlady	– Wirtin, Vermieterin
fire escape	– Feuertreppe	to nudge	– heimlich anstoßen
to peer	– spähen		

J. Nickel
Scotch

14 The Man in Black

A curl of cigarette smoke drifting upwards from behind the door showed that Nickel's visitor was still there.

"His accomplice!" hissed Frank.

Nickel suddenly looked up and saw the Black Hand Gang watching him. He drew the curtains.

"We must find out who the stranger is," said Ralph.

They went out of the yard and hid in the shadow of a wall.

There they stood for almost two hours, their patience rewarded only by the appearance of an overfed pet dog and a cat.

Finally, however, came the sound of footsteps.

A man in black slipped out of the alley and went towards a car.

"What's that in his hand," whispered Keith W. S.

"Looks like a violin case," murmured Frank.

Opening the car door, the man laid his case on the back seat and drove swiftly away. The Black Hand Gang came out of their hiding place.

"If only we'd caught a glimpse of his face!" Angela sighed.

"I did take down the car number," said Ralph.

Keith W. S. smiled: "And I know his name," he said.

What was the name of the man in black?

a curl of smoke	– eine Rauchfahne	pet dog	– Schoßhund
accomplice	– Komplize	to catch a glimpse of	– einen flüchtigen Blick erhaschen von
to reward	– belohnen		
patience	– Geduld		
overfed	– überfüttert		

BOOT AND SHOE MAKER
Nagel
1888
SEWING
ES & REPAIRS
37
VOTE
Dr. Young's
TINC
For coughs
colds and
Bronchial dis
WANTED
£500 reward
for information
leading to the
arrest of
ROBERTS
Goldrush
with
BILLY MAD
CAROLA REED
AT THE CAPITOL
16.00 and 19.00 hrs
KENYAN
Coffee
Driving Licence
Carl Rosa
SUNDAY CHRONICLE

15 A Touch of Lumbago

Keith had seen the name Carl Rosa on the driving licence in the side pocket of the car. Angela wrote the name down, and looked up, startled. "That name ..." she said.

"What about it?" Ralph asked.

"The first two letters of each word – Ca – Ro –"

"Caro," breathed Frank. "Lord Caro, Magician."

Angela put her notebook away, saying, "We know enough now to tell Sergeant Shorthouse."

At the police station they explained the whole story. Sergeant Shorthouse thought for a moment. "Where shall we find Lord Caro? I'll try the theatre."

He telephoned the theatre, but after a short conversation he put the receiver down and said, "He's at the Metropole Hotel, in bed with a touch of lumbago."

Ten minutes later they entered Lord Caro's room.

"Me having been out this afternoon?" said Lord Caro in a feeble voice. "You can see for yourselves that I'm too ill to stand."

The Sergeant saluted and apologized: "Yes, I can see that now, and I'm very sorry to have disturbed you!"

Just as they were leaving the room, Frank pulled his sleeve. "Lord Caro is lying," he whispered. "Look, he's been out not long ago."

How did Frank know Lord Caro had been out?

touch of lumbago	– Hexenschuss	feeble	– schwach
driving licence	– Führerschein	to apologize	– sich entschuldigen
startled	– erschreckt, alarmiert	to disturbe	– stören
		sleeve	– Ärmel

PALE ALE
PALE ALE
PALE ALE

16 A False Move

Sergeant Shorthouse looked at the newly filled glass of beer on the table and realized that Lord Caro was indeed lying, but he only said, “Get well soon, sir,” and left.

“Why don’t you arrest him?” Angela asked.

“Not yet,” answered the Sergeant. “We have no definite proof.”

The Black Hand Gang followed him downstairs and out into the street. Frank looked up at the window and shouted:

“He’s up!”

A shadow moved behind the curtain. Sergeant Shorthouse was pleased.

“He’ll make a false move – it’s the oldest mistake in the book,” he said. “He’ll try and run away. Watch that door.”

They watched for about twenty minutes. Suddenly Ralph cried: “That must be him!”

“Where?”

Ralph pointed down the street. “That man with the suitcases. He must have gone out of the back door.”

They ran down the side street in pursuit but they were too late.

“It’s my own fault,” said the Sergeant bitterly.

“We may find him again,” said Angela.

“We shall find him,” answered Keith W.S. confidently. “I can see him from here.”

Where was the man with the suitcases?

definite	– endgültig	in pursuit	– hier: hinterher
false move	– falsche Bewegung, Dummheit	confidently	– zuversichtlich

BEWARE
FRAUD
METROPOLE HOTEL
PAA

PAA
LB1327
VATRIX
SPARKING PLUGS
STRONG SHERRY
CASTLE STREET
EXTRA STRONG BREW
ONE WAY
WINE
2
P

17 Under the Lime Tree

The car the man from the hotel was driving had the number LB 1327. Keith W.S. recognized it as Lord Caro's car.
"Let's first go and see if he's at the theatre," said Sergeant Shorthouse. But there was no LB 1327. When they asked the porter he winked and said: "He was here. He hitched his car to the trailer and drove off with his assistant."
The Sergeant stood and thought. "He can't have gone far with that heavy trailer. We'll take my car and look for him."
They drove around for half an hour, then Angela cried:
"Stop! There he is!"
In the car park of a boarding house called *The Limes* stood the car and trailer. They tiptoed over and listened. There was no sound. Angela pointed to the roof of the trailer. "The ventilator flap is open. If we climb the tree we can see inside."
Sergeant Shorthouse and the Gang climbed the tree and the Sergeant shone his torch through the opening.
"Nothing there that looks like a stolen animal," he remarked.
"Yes, there is," said Angela. "We're looking for a panther, a parrot and a snake. One of them at least is in there and we have evidence."

Which of the animals must be in there?

lime tree	– Lindenbaum	ventilator flap	– Luftklappe Dachluke
to wink	– zwinkern	torch	– Taschenlampe
to hitch	– ankoppeln		
trailer	– Wohnwagen		

GUESTHOUSE
POLICE
POLICE

LORD CAR
THE GREAT
MAGICIAN
BIRD
SEED
PROPS

18 Perjury

Sergeant Shorthouse looked at the packet of bird seed. "Who could identify the parrot?" he asked.
"The keeper, Mr Winterton," the Gang answered.
"Good. I'll radio headquarters to send him here in a police car."
Half an hour later Mr Winterton was standing outside the trailer. He called softly: "Where's Clara?" and immediately the reply came from inside: "Clara's here. Clara's here."
"That's good enough," said the Sergeant. "Wait here."
He came back with Lord Caro and the heavily made-up assistant. "Open up!" he said.
Lord Caro obeyed and the Sergeant climbed into the trailer and opened a secret door in the wall. "My panther!" exclaimed Mr Winterton. "And the python and Clara, my little Clara!"
"Here's Clara," squawked the parrot, flapping its wings.
"Do you identify these animals?" asked Sergeant Shorthouse.
"Certainly," he replied. "These are the animals that were stolen from the zoo."
"Ridiculous!" said Lord Caro. "I bought them honestly. I know nothing about a robbery at the zoo. I'll swear to that in court."
"That will be perjury," said Ralph calmly. "You must have known about the robbery."

What had Ralph seen?

perjury	– Meineid	to flap	– schlagen mit
bird seed	– Vogelfutter	ridiculous	– lächerlich
to radio	– über Sprechfunk informieren	honestly	– auf ehrliche Weise
headquarters	– Hauptquartier	swear	– schwören
to obey	– gehorchen	in court	– vor Gericht

MAGIC
Morning
NEW THEFT AT THE ZOO

19 Conclusive Evidence

Lord Caro had the *Morning Post* in his coat pocket, so he must have known about the robbery. Sergeant Shorthouse heard his statement at the police station that night.

He said: "I bought the animals from a visiting Spaniard," and he took out a piece of paper. "This note will prove it. His name was Noratella."

Frank stepped forward. "That N could stand for Nickel," he said.

"I know no one of that name," answered Lord Caro.

"We can soon find out," said the Sergeant. "Let's go and see him."

Nickel was at home. "Just a few questions," said Sergeant Shorthouse. "You know Lord Caro?"

"Lord Caro? No, I'm afraid not."

"You deny having any dealings with him?"

"Certainly I deny it," said Nickel angrily.

"Mr Nickel is lying," said Angela quietly.

"Silly little girl!" snapped Nickel, laughing loudly.

"The proof is here in this room," said Ralph. "Mr Nickel sent that note to Lord Caro. There's no doubt about it. He's guilty."

What had Ralph seen?

conclusive	– schlüssig	to prove	– beweisen
robbery	– Diebstahl	to deny	– leugnen
statement	– Aussage	to have dealings with	– etwas zu tun haben mit
Spaniard	– Spanier	guilty	– schuldig
note	– Notiz		

FETCH PYTHON
TODAY

Calendar
PAT
Brasil

20 The Newspaper Reporter

"... I should like to thank you for your help and shall look forward to seeing you in the café at the zoo at four o'clock.
Yours sincerely, G. Sterling *Director*"
The Black Hand Gang were reading a letter. At four o'clock they were at the café to meet Mr Sterling and also the Police Superintendent who said, "You have no idea how much trouble you saved us." Mr Sterling ordered more cream cakes.
"Good afternoon, everyone," said a cheerful voice. It belonged to a young reporter from the *Evening Courier*. "Good afternoon, Mr Clarion," said the Superintendent. "Do sit down."
The reporter asked the Gang some questions.
"Three animals were stolen, is that right?"
"Yes," answered Frank. "And Nickel took them out of the zoo in his ice-cream cart?" – "Yes, and the torn-off calender in his room was conclusive evidence." Ralph added.
The reporter stared at the Gang in amazement.
Angela said: "It's not so difficult when there are five of you on the job."
"Five? But there are only four of you, aren't there?"
"No, five," said Keith W.S. "With my squirrel."
"Where is this famous squirrel?"
"Over there. Can't you see it?" said the Black Hand Gang, beginning to laugh.

Where was Keith's squirrel?

superintendent	– (Polizei-)Präsident	to tear off (tore, torn)	– abreißen
to save	– ersparen	aviary	– Vogelhaus

AVIARY
MONKEY HOUSE
52
ZOO CAFÉ
HOME BAKED CAKES OUR SPECIALITY
TO CAFÉ

21 The "Master Detectives"

Mr Clarion worked quickly. His special report appeared in the paper next day, with a photograph of them all at the café table. (Keith's squirrel, alas, was not there. It had been playing in the monkey's cage at the time.) The Black Hand Gang were reading the article quietly when Frank suddenly burst out laughing. He read: "The *Evening Courier* congratulates the master detectives of the Black Hand Gang."

How many correct answers did you score? Here is a guide to your detective ability:

to congratulate – beglückwünschen

• 1–10 correct answers:

Never mind. No man is born a master.

• 11–20 correct answers:

You have a very observant eye. If you train yourself to notice things (at home, at school and outside) you should be able to develop them still further.

• 21–29 correct answers:

You definitely have a sharp eye and one day you will certainly reach the standards of Sherlock Holmes. But don't forget that he, too, didn't stop learning throughout his life. So don't look upon doing your homework as a waste of time.

to score	– zusammenbekommen	to have a very observant eye	– eine gute Beobachtungsgabe haben
ability	– Fähigkeit	definitely	– zweifellos
		to look upon as	– ansehen als

Vocabulary

A

ability [ə'bɪlɪtɪ]	– Fähigkeit
to accelerate [ək'seləreɪt]	– beschleunigen hier: Gas geben
accomplice [ə'kɒmplɪs]	– Komplize
in advance [əd'vɑːns]	– im Voraus
alley ['ælɪ]	– Gasse, Weg hier: Torbogen
anaesthetic [ænɪs'θetɪk]	– Betäubungsmittel
ant [ænt]	– Ameise
to apologize [ə'pɒlədʒaɪz]	– sich entschuldigen
to attach [ə'tætʃ]	– festmachen
attachment [ə'tætʃmənt]	– Werkzeug
attempt [ə'temt]	– Versuch
attic ['ætɪk]	– Dachboden
audience ['ɔːdjəns]	– Zuschauer
aviary ['eɪvɪərɪ]	– Vogelhaus

B

backyard ['bækjɑːd]	– Hinterhof
bad luck [bæːd lʌk]	– Unglück, Jammer
baggage ['bægɪdʒ]	– Gepäck
bald headed ['bɔːld 'hedɪd]	– kahlköpfig
bars [bɑːz]	– Gitter
beak [biːk]	– Schnabel
to bet [bet]	– wetten
to betray [bɪ'treɪ]	– verraten
to bicker ['bɪkə]	– zetern
to book [bʊk]	– buchen, vorbestellen

bottom ['bɒtəm]	– Grund
to brake [breɪk]	– bremsen
to brush [brʌʃ]	– bürsten, wischen hier: vorbeisausen
bunny rabbit ['bʌnɪ'ræbɪt]	– Karnickel
burglary ['bɜːglərɪ]	– Einbruch

C

camp site ['kæmpsaɪt]	– Campingplatz
cart [kɑːt]	– Wagen, Karre
case [keɪs]	– Fall
to catch the ear	– zu hören sein
to catch a glimpse of [glɪmps]	– einen flüchtigen Blick erhaschen
to check [tʃek]	– überprüfen, auswerten
check trousers ['traʊzəz]	– karierte Hosen
to cheer up [tʃɪə]	– aufmuntern
cheroot [ʃə'ruːt]	– Stumpen
to clasp [klɑːsp]	– (er)greifen hier: halten, stützen
clue [kluː]	– Spur, Beweis
coin [kɔɪn]	– Münze
to collect [kə'lekt]	– (an)sammeln hier: abholen
to comb [kəʊm]	– durchkämmen
to come across [kʌm ə'krɒs]	– stoßen auf …
commissionaire [kə'mɪʃə'neə]	– Portier
to complain [kəm'pleɪn]	– sich beklagen
conclusive [kən'kluːsɪv]	– schlüssig
confidently ['kɒnfɪdəntlɪ]	– zuversichtlich
to congratulate [kən'grætjʊleɪt]	– beglückwünschen

to contain [kən'teɪn]	– enthalten
in court [kɔːt]	– vor Gericht
creaking ['kriːkɪŋ]	– krächzend
crowd [kraʊd]	– Menschenmenge
curl of smoke [kɜːləv sməʊk]	– Rauchfahne
curly ['kɜːlɪ]	– lockig
curtly ['kɜːtlɪ]	– schroff
to cycle ['saɪkl]	– Rad fahren

D

damage ['dæmɪdʒ]	– Schaden
(to have) dealings with [diːlɪŋz]	– etwas zu tun haben mit
definite ['defɪnɪt]	– endgültig
to deny [dɪ'nai]	– leugnen
description [dɪs'krɪpʃn]	– Beschreibung
to develop [dɪ'veləp]	– entwickeln
to dial ['daɪəl]	– wählen
(to be in) difficulties ['dɪfɪkəltiːz]	– Schwierigkeiten (haben)
disgraceful [dɪs'greɪsfʊl]	– schändlich
to dispose of [dɪs'pəʊz]	– loswerden
to disturb [dɪs'tɜːb]	– stören
doorhandle ['dɔːhændl]	– Türklinke
to doubt [daʊt]	– bezweifeln
driving licence ['draɪvɪŋ'laɪsəns]	– Führerschein

E

to emerge [ɪ'mɜːdʒ]	– hervorkommen
to enable [ɪ'neɪbl]	– in die Lage versetzen
enclosure [ɪn'kloʊʒə]	– Gehege
to equip [ɪ'kwɪp]	– ausstatten

to establish [ɪs'tæblɪʃ]	– gründen, schaffen hier: feststellen
ether ['ɪθə]	– Äther
evidence ['evɪdəns]	– Beweisstück
exasperated [ɪg'zɑːspəreɪtɪd]	– wütend
exchange [ɪks'tʃeɪndʒ]	– (Fernsprech-) Amt
excitement [ɪk'saɪtmənt]	– Aufregung
exit ['eksɪt]	– Ausgang

F

faded ['feɪdɪd]	– verblichen
faint [feɪnt]	– schwach
false move [fɒːls muːv]	– falsche Bewegung, Dummheit
fate [feɪt]	– Schicksal
fault [fɔːlt]	– Fehler
feather ['feðə]	– Feder
feeble ['fiːbl]	– schwach
fingerprint ['fɪŋgəprɪnt]	– Fingerabdruck
fire escape ['faɪərɪs'keɪp]	– Feuertreppe
to fit [fɪt]	– passen (auf)
to flag [flæg]	– stocken, weniger werden
(ventilator–) flap [('ventɪleɪtə) flæp]	– Luftklappe, Dachluke
flat [flæt]	– Wohnung
flipper ['flɪpə]	– Flosse
frogman ['frɒgmən]	– Froschmann, Taucher
front row [frʌnt rəʊ]	– vordere Reihe
furiously ['fjʊərɪəsli]	– wütend

G

gang [gæŋ]	– Bande
to gaze at [geɪz]	– genau anschauen

gear [gɪə] – Ausrüstung, Sachen hier: Kleidung
to get up to some funny tricks – lustige Einfälle haben
to give oneself away – sich verraten
gloom [glu:m] – Dunkelheit
glove [glʌv] – Handschuh
gone [gɔn] – verschwunden
to grin [grɪn] – grinsen
to grunt [grʌnt] – brummen
guilty ['gɪltɪ] – schuldig

H

handcuffs ['hændkʌfs] – Handschellen
handprint ['hændprɪnt] – Handabdruck
headquarters ['hed'kwɔ:təz] – Hauptquartier
(thank) heavens! [θæŋk'hevnz] – Gott sei Dank!
heavily made up ['hevɪlɪ] – aufgedonnert
heirloom ['eəlu:m] – Erbstück
to hesitate ['hezɪteɪt] – zögern
to hitch [hitʃ] – ankoppeln
honestly ['ɔnɪstlɪ] – auf ehrliche Weise

I

to imitate ['ɪmɪteɪt] – nachahmen
including [ɪn'klu:dɪŋ] – samt
inflammable [ɪn'flæməbl] – brennbar
innocently ['ɪnəsntlɪ] – unschuldig
inseparable [ɪn'sepərəbl] – unzertrennlich
to introduce ['ɪntrədju:s] – vorstellen

J

jewellery ['dʒu:əlrɪ] – Schmuck

L

lake [leɪk] – See
landlady ['lændleɪdɪ] – Wirtin, Vermieterin
to latch [lætʃ] – anlehnen
lawn [lɔːn] – Rasen
leader ['liːdə] – Anführer
to lend a hand [lend ə hænd] – mithelfen
to lie [laɪ] – lügen
likely ['laɪklɪ] – wahrscheinlich
lime tree ['laɪm trɪː] – Lindenbaum
limply ['lɪmplɪ] – schlaff
lodge [lɒdʒ] – Pförtnerloge
to loiter ['lɔitə] – trödeln, sich herumtreiben
hier: herumschlendern
loot [luːt] – Beute
to look upon as [lʊk ə'pɒn] – ansehen als
(their) luck was in [lʌk] – sie hatten Glück

M

magician [mə'dʒɪʃŋ] – Zauberkünstler
magnifying-glass['mægnɪfaɪŋ] – Vergrößerungsglas
mail [meɪl] – Post(sendung)
mobile unit ['məʊbaɪl'juːnɪt] – Rollkommando
mock politeness ['mɒk pə'laɪtnɪs] – übertriebene Höflichkeit
to mow [məʊ] – mähen

N

necklace ['neklɪs] – Halskette
note [nəʊt] – Notiz
to nudge [nʌdʒ] – heimlich anstoßen
(what a) nuisance ['njuːsns] – wie ärgerlich
number plate ['nʌmbəpleɪt] – Nummernschild

O

to obey [ə'beɪ] – gehorchen
to object ['əb'dʒekt] – Einspruch erheben
to observe [əb'zɜːv] – beobachten
odd [ɒd] – komisch
overfed ['əʊvə'fed] – überfüttert

P

package ['pækɪdʒ] – Paket
painting ['peɪntɪŋ] – Bild, Gemälde
parrot ['pærət] – Papagei
patience ['peɪʃns] – Geduld
to pedal off ['pedl] – in die Pedale treten
peephole ['piːphəʊl] – Guckloch
to peer [pɪə] – spähen
penknife ['pennaɪf] – Taschenmesser
perjury ['pɜːdʒərɪ] – Meineid
pet dog ['pet 'dɒg] – Schoßhund
pigeon loft ['pɪdʒɪn lɒft] – Taubenschlag
to pin to [pɪn] – anheften an
to point out [pɔɪnt] – hinweisen auf
to poke [pəʊk] – stoßen
power of observation [ɒbzə'veɪʃn] – Beobachtungsgabe
preserving glass [prɪ'zɜːvɪŋ glɑːs] – Einmachglas
to pretend [prɪ'tend] – vortäuschen
probably ['prɒbəblɪ] – vermutlich
profession [prə'feʃn] – Beruf
professional [prə'feʃnl] – von einem Fachmann
proof [pruːf] – Beweis

props [prɒps] – Requisiten
to prove [pruːv] – beweisen
pseudonym ['sjuːdənɪm] – Künstlername, Pseudonym

to pump up [pʌmp] – aufpumpen
in pursuit [pə'sjuːt] – hinterher(-rennen)
python (snake) ['paɪθən] – Pythonschlange

Q

quick–witted ['kwɪk-'wɪtɪd] – schlagfertig

R

to race off [reɪs] – davonrasen
to radio ['reɪdɪəʊ] – über Sprechfunk informieren
to raise [reɪz] – heben, verbessern
to realize ['rɪəlaɪz] – (be)merken
rear wheel [rɪə wiːl] – Hinterrad
to recognize ['rekəgnaɪz] – wieder erkennen
to recover [rɪ'kʌvə] – wieder finden
reed [riːd] – Schilf
reverse side [rɪ'vəːs saɪd] – Rückseite
to reward [rɪ'wɔːd] – belohnen
ridiculous [rɪ'dɪkjʊləs] – lächerlich
robbery ['rɔbərɪ] – Diebstahl
rope [rəʊp] – Leine
(front–)row [rəʊ] – vordere Reihe

S

safety lock ['seɪftɪ 'lɔk] – Sicherheitsschloss
to save [seɪf] – ersparen
to saw, sawed, sawn [sɔː] – sägen
score [skɔː] – Punktzahl, Trefferzahl
to score – zusammenbekommen
scornful ['skɔːnfʊl] – in verächtlichem Ton
to screech [skriːtʃ] – kreischen
to search [sɜːtʃ] – durchsuchen
searching stare [steə] – forschend anblicken
to separate ['sepəreɪt] – sich trennen

sergeant ['sɑːdʒnt]	– Wachtmeister
to settle [setl]	– sich niederlassen
sharp [ʃɑːp]	– scharf, spitz hier: gute
shelter ['ʃeltə]	– Unterschlupf
to shore away [ʃɔː]	– fortscheuchen
shutter ['ʃʌtə]	– Verschluss
to signal ['sɪgnl]	– signalisieren
silence ['saɪləns]	– Stille
skill [skɪl]	– Geschicklichkeit
sleeve [sliːv]	– Ärmel
to slip out [slɪp]	– sich hinausstehlen
slot [slɒt]	– Einwurf, Schlitz
snake [sneɪk]	– Schlange
to snap at [snæp]	– schnappen
Spaniard ['spænjəd]	– Spanier
(high) spirits [spɪrɪts]	– gute Stimmung
to spoil [spɔɪl]	– verderben
(on the) spot [spɒt]	– zur Stelle
to spot	– entdecken
to spring [sprɪŋ]	– springen, ausgelöst werden hier: zuschnappen
to squawk [skwɔːk]	– kreischen
squealing ['skwiːlɪŋ]	– Quietschen
to squint [skwɪnt]	– herumgucken
squirrel ['skwɪrəl]	– Eichhörnchen
statement ['steɪtmənt]	– Aussage
startled [stɑːtld]	– erschreckt
to state [steɪt]	– darlegen, vortragen hier: feststellen
sternly [stɜːnli]	– streng

store cupboards ['stɔːkʌbədz]	– Vorratsschränke
to stream [striːm]	– strömen
to stroll up [strəʊl]	– heranschlendern
stunned [stʌnd]	– betäubt
to sue [sjuː]	– verklagen
to suggest [sə'dʒest]	– vorschlagen, meinen
superintendant [sjuːperɪn'tendənt]	– (Polizei)–Präsident
to surface ['sɜːfɪs]	– an die Oberfläche kommen
surface	– Oberfläche
suspect [səs'pekt]	– der Verdächtige
suspicious [sə'spɪʃəs]	– verdächtig
to swear [sweə]	– schwören
sweat [swet]	– Schweiß
to sweep [swiːp]	– fegen, jagen

T

to take a stroll [strəʊl]	– einen Streifengang machen
tape-recorder [teɪp'rɪ'kɔːdə]	– Tonbandgerät
to tear (tore, torn) [teə, tɔː, tɔːn]	– abreißen
theft [θeft]	– Diebstahl
though [ðəʊ]	– jedoch
thread [θred]	– Bindfaden
throbbing ['θrɒbɪŋ]	– Dröhnen
to tiptoe ['tɪp'təʊ]	– auf Zehenspitzen gehen
tire ['taɪə]	– Reifen
torch [tɔːtʃ]	– Taschenlampe
touch of lumbago [tʌtʃəvlʌm'beɪgəʊ]	– Hexenschuss
trace [treɪs]	– Spur
trade name [treɪd neɪm]	– Warenzeichen
to track down [træk]	– zur Strecke bringen

trail [treɪl] – Fährte
trailer ['treɪlə] – Wohnwagen
trap [træp] – Falle
trap door ['træp'dɔː] – Bodenklappe, Falltür
to treat [triːt] – behandeln
hier: präparieren
trolley ['trɒlɪ] – Wagen
trunk call [trʌnk kɔl] – Ferngespräch
tug [tʌg] – Ruck

U

undoubtedly [ʌn'daʊtɪdlɪ] – ohne Zweifel
unison ['juːnɪzn] – gleichzeitig
unnoticed [ʌn'nəʊtɪst] – unbeobachtet
to unscrew ['ʌn'skruː] – abschrauben
to upset [ʌp'set] – verwirren
urgent [ɜːdʒnt] – dringend
(no) use [juːs] – nutzlos

V

to vanish ['vænɪʃ] – verschwinden
ventriloquist [ven'trɪləkwɪst] – Bauchredner
vet. (veterinary surgeon) [vet] [('vetnrɪ 'sɜːdʒən)] – Tierarzt
vicious ['vɪʃəs] – bösartig

W

to waggle ['wægl] – wackeln
to wake [weɪk] – aufwecken
waste of time [weɪstəvtaɪm] – Zeitvergeudung
(to keep a close) watch [wɒtʃ] – genau beobachten
to wink [wɪŋk] – zwinkern

Lies mich ...

Englisch lernen mit Witzen

"I say, waiter, this water is cloudy!"
"The water's all right, Sir, it's the glass that's dirty."

Mick: "My brother is very unusual. He does farmyard impressions."
Nick: "What's unusual about that?"
Mick: "He doesn't do the sounds, he does the smells ..."

Vicar: "You must not fight, little boy. You should love your enemy."
Boy: "But he's not my enemy. He's my brother."

Jack: "Our dog is just like one of the family."
Jill: "Really? Which one?"

Angry teacher: "Why are you so late?"
Lazy pupil: "Well, I saw the sign in the street that said "School ahead – go slow"!"

Patient: "Doctor, my family thinks I'm mad."
Doctor: "Why?"
Patient: "Because I like sausages."
Doctor: "Nonsense, I like sausages too."
Patient: "You do? You must come round and see my collection. I have hundreds."

"Waiter, there's no chicken in this chicken pie."
"So what, Sir, you don't get dog in a dog biscuit."

It was two o'clock in the morning when Fred phoned Joe. The phone rang for hours before it was picked up and Joe's sleepy voice said, "Hello?"
"Sorry to get you out of bed at this time of night," said Fred.
"That's all right," said Joe, "I had to get up anyway to answer the phone."

"Hands up all those who want to go to Heaven," said the Sunday School teacher.
Everyone put their hands up except Kenneth.
"Don't you want to got to Heaven, Kenneth?"
"I can't, Miss," said Kenneth. "My mum told me to come straight home."

"Mum, now that I'm fifteen, can I wear eye-shadow and lipstick and mascara and perfume and wear high-heeled shoes?"
"No, Charles, you may not."

What's yellow on the inside and green on the outside?
A banana disguised as a cucumber.

Then there was the Irish helicopter pilot who crashed.
He thought it was too cold so he turned the fan off.

Then there was the Irishman whose sister had a baby. Nobody told him if it was a boy or a girl so he didn't know if he was an uncle or an aunt.

Teacher: "Give me a sentence starting with 'I', Nicholas."
Nicholas: "Yes, Sir. 'I' is –"
Teacher: "No, no, Nicholas! You don't say 'I is', you say 'I am'."
Nicholas: "All right, Sir. I am the ninth letter of the alphabet."

"I'd like some crocodile shoes, please."
"Certainly, madam, what size are your crocodiles?"

Tommy's father rushed out of the bathroom waving his shaving brush. "This thing's useless!" he complained. "I can't shave with it."
"That's funny," said Tommy. "It was fine this morning when I washed my bike with it."

"I dont't care who you are; get your reindeer off my roof!"

"Is this Juster's Cheese Store?"
"Yes, Ma'am."
"What do you do with a smelly cheese when it's a year old?"
"Wish it a happy birthday."

What's the best way to catch a rabbit?
Hide in a bush and make a noise like a lettuce.

Mother: "Aunt Edna won't kiss you with that dirty face."
Johnny: "That's just what I was up to."

Mother: "Eat your spinach, dear. It will put colour into your cheeks."
Johnny: "Who wants to have green cheeks?"

"Doctor, doctor, everyone keeps ignoring me."
"Next patient, please!"

"Waiter, waiter, the service here is terrible."
"If you think the service is terrible, wait until you see the food!"

"Is your mother at home?"
"Well, you don't think I'm mowing the lawn because I want to, do you?"

A little girl was playing in the park, when a kindly old lady started talking to her.
"And do you go to school ?" she asked.
"No," was the sulky answer, "I'm sent!"

Doctor: "Are you still taking the cough medicine I gave you?"
Patient: "No. I tasted it once and decided that I'd rather have the cough."

How can you tell which end of the worm is its head?
Tickle its middle and see which end smiles.

"Did you miss me while I was gone?"
"Were you gone?"

He (at the cinema): "Can you see all right?"
She: "Yes."
He: "You're not sitting in a draught?"
She: "No."
He: "Comfortable seat?"
She: "Yes, fine."
He: "Mind changing places?"

Bobby: "Dad, are you still growing?"
Dad: "No, of course not. Why?"
Bobby: "Well, the top of your head is beginning to push through your hair."

How can you tell if there's been an elephant in your fridge?
There'll be footprints in the butter.

"Did you take my advice about your sleeplessness? Did you count sheep?"
"Yes, I did, doctor. I counted up to 482,347."
"And did you fall asleep?"
"No – it was time to get up!"

"Dad, where are the Himalayas?"
"Ask your mother. She puts everything away."

Mother: "Come in, Darren, and I'll give you some chocolate biscuits. Are your feet dirty?"
Darren: "Yes, Mum, but I've got my shoes on."

How can we be sure that Santa Claus is an Irishman? Usually there are two doors in a house and eight windows and he goes down the chimney.

How do you keep an idiot in suspense?
I'll tell you tomorrow.

First policeman: "The thief got away then? Did you put guards on all the exits?"
Second policeman: "Of course we did. But he tricked us and went out through the entrance."

"How old are you now, Darren?" asked his auntie. "How do you mean?" answered Darren. „When I'm on a bus, when I go to the cinema, or in real life?"

A car-driver stopped in a small village and called to a passer-by, "Excuse me, can you tell me where this road goes to?"
"It doesn't go anywhere," grinned the local. "It stays right where it is."

Did you hear about the man who went to see the optician because he saw spots in front of his eyes?
The optician gave him glasses, and now he can see the spots much better.

Teacher: "What happened to your homework?"
Jerry: "I made it into a paper plane, and somebody hijacked it!"

"Care to come to my birthday party on Saturday, Jill!"
"Thanks, Trevor. Where do you live?"
"Number thirty-eight, London Road. Just push the bell with your elbow."
"Why with my elbow?"
"You're not coming empty-handed, are you?"